OTTERS UNDER WATER

Jim Arnosky

G. P. Putnam's Sons

New York

G. P. Putnam's Sons, a division of The Putnam & Grosset Group,
200 Madison Avenue, New York, NY 10016.
Published simultaneously in Canada.
Printed in Hong Kong by South China Printing Co. (1988) Ltd.
Book design by Nanette Stevenson and Colleen Flis.
The text was set in Goudy Old Style.
Library of Congress Cataloging-in-Publication Data
Arnosky, Jim. Otters under water/by Jim Arnosky. p.   cm.
Summary: Shows two young otters frolicking and feeding in a pond.
1. Otters—Juvenile literature.   [1. Otters.]   I. Title.   II. Title: Otters
under water. QL737.C25A76   1992   599.74'447—dc20   91-36792 CIP AC
ISBN 0-399-22339-8
1 3 5 7 9 10 8 6 4 2
First Impression

It is morning and the sun
is shining softly on the pond.

Two young otters glide by,
making ripples on the water.

swimming in a line,

rolling on their backs,

From the bank, the mother otter
watches her pups...

swimming side by side,

holding their breath,
then diving.

Underwater, they hunt for fish

and crayfish.

They see newts

and snapping turtles.

Otters can hold their breath
a long time. The two sneak
under floating ducks.

They follow slow muskrats.

Otters can swim fast!
One pup chases a yellow perch.

The other pup catches
a silver minnow.

Then, at once, the pups
pop up to the surface to breathe

and find their mother still
watching from the bank.

It is morning and the sun
is shining softly.